Introducing
Lucy Richards

When I was seven I had great
fun making this snow woman.
There wasn't much snow, so she
wasn't very big – but she did
look brilliant in my Auntie
Polly's favourite pink hat!

This book belongs to

_____

The magic sky that Rory sees in this story is a real phenomenon.
It can be seen in the Arctic and far northern hemisphere and is called
the Aurora Borealis, or Northern Lights.

The lights appear to move across the sky and are often described
as natural fireworks. They can vary in colour from greens,
pinks and purples to reds. When the lights are a red

Although the Northern Lights occur all year round, they can
best be seen in early spring and late autumn – because during
the summer months, the nights are too light to see them.

So perhaps one day you will travel to the Arctic and see
the Northern Lights for yourself!

Dedicated to Mum, Jenny and Sean – you are stars!

A big thank you to Suzanne, Susan and Frances.

Lucy Richards would like to acknowledge the children at Newton Prep
for their help and enthusiasm.

First published 2004
By Egmont Books Limited
239 Kensington High Street, London W8 6SA
Text and Illustrations copyright © Lucy Richards 2004
Lucy Richards has asserted her moral rights
1 4052 1334 5 hb
1 4052 1335 3 pb
7 9 10 8 6
Printed in China

The Magic Sky

Lucy Richards

EGMONT

"Why do I always have to go to bed early?" asked Rory.
"I'm not tired."

"Soon we'll stay up late and see the magic sky," said Mum.
"But right now it's time to go to sleep."

The next morning
when Rory woke up,
he was very excited.

"When will we see the magic sky?" he asked.

"After five more bedtimes," said Mum.
"We have to go fishing first."

Dad took Rory fishing on the ice.
Rory waited a **long** time but he didn't catch any fish.

The next day Rory said, "When will we see the magic sky?"

"Not for four more bedtimes," said Dad.
"We have lots of work to do first."

So Dad took Rory outside to collect some wood.

"You are a very
strong bear!"
he laughed, as they
walked home.

When Rory woke up the next morning, he said,
"When will we see the magic sky?"

"After three more bedtimes," said Mum.
"You've got plenty of time to play with your friends first."

So Rory played . . . and played . . . and played.

Sledging was the most fun!

wheeeee!

When Rory woke up the next morning, he said,
"When will we see the magic sky?"

"Not for two more bedtimes," said Mum.
"There's time for us to go exploring first."

Mum and Rory walked and ran until their legs
were worn out. They saw lots of wonderful things.

The next morning Rory was getting bored with waiting.
"When will we see the magic sky?" he asked.

"After one more bedtime," said Dad.
"There's time for you to learn to swim first."

SPLOOSH! went Rory, into the icy water.

Then there was a HUGE splash and Dad dived in.

"Swim, Rory, swim!" he said.

Rory followed Dad, paddling hard.

The next morning Rory asked,
"When will we see the magic sky?"

"Tonight!" said Mum.
"We'll see the magic sky tonight!"

"HURRAY!" cried Rory.
"I can't wait!" And he rushed off to play.

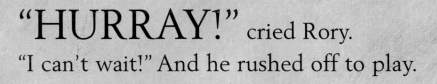

"Let's go and see the magic sky now!"
Rory said to his friends.

But they were busy making snow bears, so he went on his own.

Rory ran and ran looking for the magic sky.
But as he ran, the snow fell faster and the wind blew harder.

He couldn't see the magic sky and now he was lost and all ALONE!

Just as Rory was thinking he would **never** be found,

he heard a muffled sound behind him.

"Mum!" he shouted, in relief.

"What are you doing on your own?" she said.
"I was looking for the magic sky!" replied Rory.

"Oh, Rory," said Mum. "We have to wait for night-time first!"
So Mum and Rory tramped back home through the snow.

Soon it was getting dark. "Now it's time to go and see
the magic sky!" said Mum.

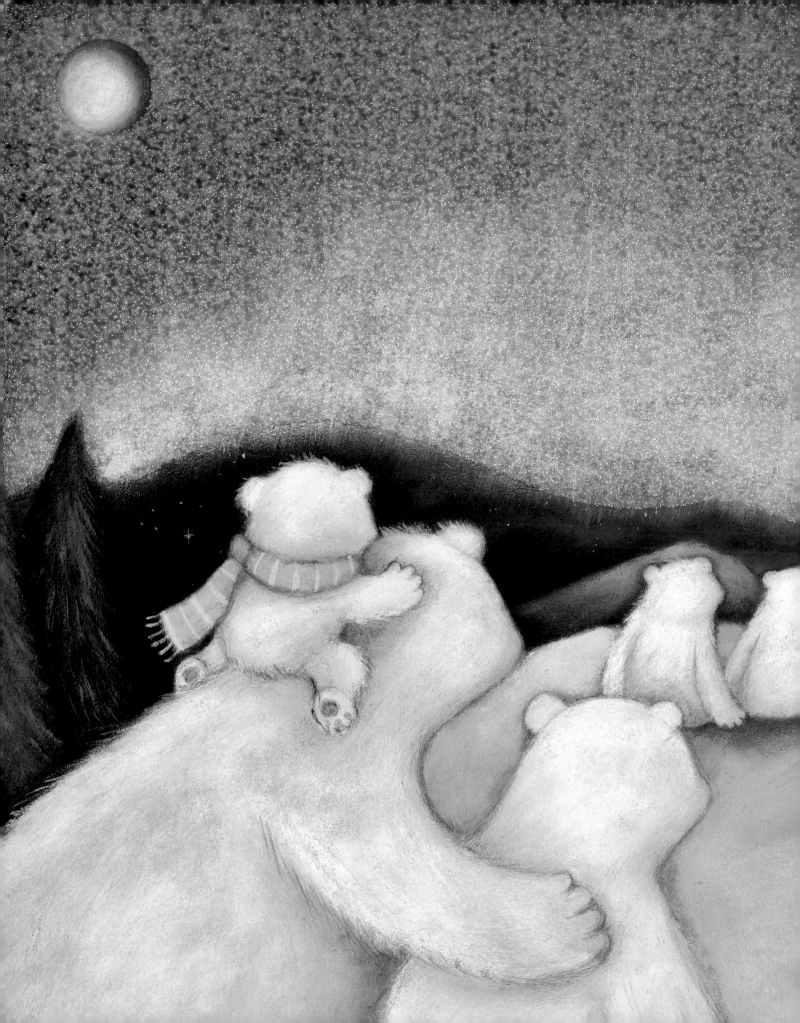

They all went out into the cold night.
"Look at all the colours moving in the sky," said Mum.
"They're called the Northern Lights," said Dad.
"OOOhhh," yawned Rory, happily. "It really is MAGIC!"

"It has been a very exciting day hasn't it, Rory?" whispered Mum. "Now it's definitely time for bed!"

This time Rory didn't argue . . . he was already drifting off to sleep, dreaming about his magic sky.

Enjoy more beautiful books
from
Lucy Richards

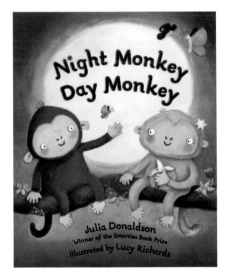

Night Monkey, Day Monkey
Julia Donaldson and Lucy Richards

Night Monkey and Day Monkey's worlds
are as different as . . . night and day!
In learning about each other's opposite worlds,
they also learn to be the best of friends.

ISBN 0 7497 4893 1 (paperback)

Mairi's Mermaid
Michael Morpurgo and Lucy Richards

Robbie says swimming is easy. You just have to pretend
you're a mermaid. But that doesn't help Mairi.
She isn't even sure that mermaids are real . . .

ISBN 0 7497 4272 0 (paperback)